A LITTLE HORSE
CALLED PANCAKES
AND THE BEACH RESCUE

Written by Candice Noakes-Dobson
Illustrated by Wendy Paterson

To Anna B, John, Ruby, Lucy, Ella Murphy and family. Without all your guidance and support, none of this would be possible.
And to all who are part of the SARDA family, thank you.
You transform lives every day.

The South African Riding for the Disabled Association (S.A.R.D.A.), was established in Cape Town in 1973 by Belinda Sampson and Joy Finlay. Today there are branches in Durban, Port Elizabeth and on the Highveld. SARDA is affiliated to the RDA in the United Kingdom and the Federation for Disabled Riding International. SARDA's aim is to provide the opportunity of therapeutic and recreational horse riding for disabled people so that they might benefit in all aspects of their mental, physical and social lives.
The branch exists as a result of teamwork with all instructors and helpers volunteering their time and knowledge.

email:
national@sarda.co.za

Little Annabel (Anna B, for short) lived at Sweet Valley Farm in Cape Town on the tip of Africa.

Sweet Valley Farm was a happy farm full of baby chicks, hens, ducks, cats, dogs, horses, ponies and an extra-special miniature horse called Pancakes.

Anna B took care of all her animals. She particularly loved spring when her hen, Henny Penny, would disappear into the garage and find a quiet place on the top shelf of the storage shelves. She would lay her eggs in the box Anna B had placed there, and sit on them for twenty-one days.

Anna B would mark the days off on a calendar, and on the twenty-first day would rush through to quietly listen for the newly hatched chicks.

The next day Anna B would carefully move Henny Penny and her just-hatched chicks to a coop near her bedroom so she could keep an eye on them. She had to do this before the chicks became too mobile, otherwise they could fall off the shelf and hurt themselves.

During the day Henny Penny and her chicks would roam the garden eating bugs and taking dust baths. Pancakes loved the baby chicks. In the afternoon, once Anna B had taken him from his paddock back to his stable to spend the night, he would let the chicks come in and join him for a little while.

When Anna B had finished her chores, she would march the chicks to their coop to settle for the night. That way they wouldn't end up as dinner for the wild caracal cat that roamed the valley at night.

Spring brought new life to the valley and the majestic mountains that overlooked the farm. Badly burnt by the summer wild fires, they were now showing patches of green and beautiful fynbos flowers were beginning to bloom. Pancakes had been devastated by the way the fire burnt all the plants, and was delighted that the land was healing.

Every spring SARDA hosts a showjumping event in lovely
Noordhoek to raise funds. Anna B was excited because she
had earned enough pocket money over the holidays to enter
Candy Floss into the showjumping and Pancakes into the
fancy-dress competition at the show.

  To get to Noordhoek you have to drive over Anna B's
beloved mountain on a road called Ou Kaapse Weg.
You can look down on the whole town and see the beautiful
beaches surrounding the Cape Peninsula.

Candy Floss had been very nervous after a tree fell down near her and her reins got caught in the bushes during the summer fires. Anna B and Pancakes had worked hard to help her regain her confidence. A friend of her mom's called Jenku, an expert in training horses, came to the farm to help.

Jenku taught Anna B and Pancakes to be patient with Candy Floss, and told them to praise her for what she did right and not to get cross with her when she did something wrong.

Jenku gave them an exercise, walking between two drums. At first Candy Floss was scared and didn't want to do it. Pancakes, who was watching from the side of the paddock, saw Candy Floss struggling so he trotted through the drums to encourage his friend. Anna B gave Candy Floss a small treat for every positive step she took towards the drums.

Over three weeks, Candy Floss's trust grew so much that Anna B and Pancakes could even put a tyre between the drums and she was able to walk over it. Soon Anna B was able to climb on her back and, with Pancakes leading, Candy Floss would trot over the tyre. Eventually Candy Floss got so brave she could jump over two tyres on her own.

Jenku also taught Anna B and Pancakes about having a safe place when they went to shows. They needed something that Candy Floss could stand on, which could easily be folded up and taken to shows. Pancakes immediately thought of the waterproof picnic blanket and went to find it.

Pancakes then taught Candy Floss to stand and relax on the blanket. She began to feel safe and secure on it. This was important, as horse shows can be frightening, with new sights, sounds, smells and other horses. While on the blanket, Candy Floss's body relaxed and her head lowered. As Anna B knew, when a horse's head lowers it immediately feels calmer.

Finally, it was the day before the show - time to bath the ponies and pack the horsebox. Anna B had a long list of things to pack. Luckily for her, Pancakes loved helping.

The list included a saddle, a numnah (which goes under the saddle to prevent it from rubbing the pony's back), a bridle, grooming brushes, water buckets, hay nets, spare halters, a first-aid kit, riding clothes, a helmet and the costume for Pancakes.

As the theme of the show was 'Spring', Anna B had decorated Pancakes's bridle with beautiful flowers and brought some extra ones along to plait into his mane and tail. She had also made some butterflies from pipe cleaners and tissue paper. Anna B was herself going to be dressed as a bumblebee when she led Pancakes.

Very early the next morning, Candy Floss, Pancakes, Anna B and her parents headed off to the show.

The jumping class was first. Anna B and Candy Floss had a perfect clear round and won a purple rosette. Anna B gave Candy Floss a big hug because she was so proud of her for not being scared of any of the jumps.

While they waited for the fancy-dress class to begin, Anna B and the ponies stood to the side of the show arena watching as the jumps got bigger and the riders older. Candy Floss didn't even need to stand on her safe picnic blanket because she was feeling so secure with Pancakes by her side.

The next rider announced was Ella, on Spice Girl. The most beautiful chestnut pony entered the arena with a young girl on her back. Anna B and Pancakes could not believe this girl could jump so high and with such control. She was so kind to her pony, giving her a huge hug after a clear round of jumping. Anna B hoped that if she practised really hard, she would be able to ride just like Ella one day.

Pancakes nudged Anna B. It was time for them to get ready for the fancy-dress competition.

The announcer's voice suddenly came over the loudspeaker: 'Attention, ladies and gentlemen! A dog has gone missing. Please look out for a cream toy Pomeranian belonging to the show judge. Bernadette was last seen sleeping in her basket in the club house. Please report urgently to the announcer's stand if you have any information.'

Pancakes remembered something: while he and Anna B watched Ella jump, he had seen a little dog running down a path beside the arena.

How could he let Anna B know? Pancakes tugged at her sleeve. She thought he wanted a carrot or snack, but he kept at it until she said, 'Pancakes, what are you trying to tell me?' He trotted to the path beside the arena, looking behind him to make sure Anna B was following.

Anna B didn't know where the path led. As it happened, Ella was getting ready for the fancy-dress competition next to their horsebox. 'Ella, where does this path lead to?' she asked. 'We think the missing dog may have gone this way.'
 'To the beach,' said Ella. 'Oh dear. You'd better hurry because the beach is very long and that little dog could easily get lost. If the the tide changes she could even get swept out to sea. Shall I come with you?'

Ella jumped on Spice Girl's back. Anna B was on Candy Floss and Pancakes followed behind. They trotted down a path which opened onto the most beautiful beach of white sand, but it was huge, stretching along the coast in both directions. Which way should they go?

On the right, the beach led to a distant rocky cliff. On the left, they could see a big shipwreck partially buried in the sand. Ella's brother was on the beach, fishing with his friends.

'Connor, we're looking for the show judge's dog, Bernadette,' Ella said. 'She's gone missing. Have you seen her?'

'She's a tiny dog, a toy Pomeranian,' said Anna B.

'Well, I did see a small dog follow some bigger dogs to the wreck,' said Connor. 'I thought the little dog was part of the pack. Is she light coloured?'

'Yes, she's cream! That must be her!' said Anna B.

Ella and Anna B trotted quickly up the beach towards the wreck. Anna B thought it looked scary and was worried that Candy Floss would be spooked. Ella reassured her that she had trained her pony on the beach, and that if Candy Floss followed Spice Girl, and Pancakes went behind her, she would feel safe.

Pancakes had so much fun trotting through the waves that he almost forgot they were on a mission, but he soon remembered when he heard a forlorn bark coming from the direction of the wreck.

When they got to the wreck, it was much bigger than Pancakes or Anna B could have imagined. The tide was coming in and they needed to be quick to avoid being swept out to sea. They could hear faint yelps coming from inside the wreck. Ella jumped off Spice Girl and searched frantically for Bernadette while Anna B kept an eye out for the incoming tide.

Eventually Ella spotted little Bernadette, cold and huddled in a corner of the rusty wreck. The other dogs had gone. The tiny dog had crawled into a part of the wreck through a hole when the tide was low. Now it was filling up and she was too afraid to swim through to get out. It wasn't safe for the girls to go into the wreck, so they came up with an idea. If they could make some kind of basket and lower it into the wreck, then Bernadette could climb into it and they could hoist her out to safety.

Using her jacket and the reins off Candy Floss's bridle, Anna B constructed a kind of basket. Ella then stood on Pancakes's back and lowered it down. After a few nervous seconds – yes! – Bernadette jumped onto the makeshift basket. Ella hoisted her out of the wreck while Anna B cheered.

The sea water was swirling around the girls' feet and the ponies' hooves. Ella grabbed Bernadette, gave Anna B back her reins and jersey and jumped onto Spice Girl. Then Bernadette jumped out of Ella's arms onto Pancakes's back. Just in time! They had to canter away from the wreck to escape the incoming tide.

   Passing Connor as they headed back, they called out, 'We found her! Thank you!'

When the girls arrived back at the showground, the fancy-dress competition was about to start. They rushed to get changed. Bernadette refused to get off Pancakes's back, so they decided she should be part of the fancy-dress show too. Anna B rustled around in her costume box and, with a little tweaking, came up with something for Bernadette to wear.

Spice Girl and Ella led the way into the arena. Ella was a flower fairy and Spice Girl wore a beautiful blanket covered in flowers. Pancakes, Anna B and Bernadette entered next. The judge could not believe her eyes when she saw Bernadette, safe and sound, riding on the back of Pancakes dressed as a ladybird!

The ponies were awarded beautiful rosettes for their costumes and for raising money to buy new riding hats and boots for the children who ride at SARDA. The judge also congratulated the ponies and girls for working as a team to rescue her dog. She picked Bernadette off Pancakes's back and hugged her tight, then gave Pancakes an extra-special pat.

Later, as Anna B loaded Candy Floss and Pancakes into their horsebox, she heard a little cheep. She couldn't believe it: perched on Pancakes's hay net were four baby chicks! They must have sneaked in when they left home that morning. Anna B gave each pony a carrot and a hug, and thanked them for doing their best and for being her best friends.

Anna B put some hay in her riding helmet, then placed the chicks inside and sat with them on her lap as they drove back over the mountain to reunite them with Henny Penny. As she looked down at the sleeping chicks on her lap, she smiled and thought, 'Spring really is a special time of year!'

The end

Candice Noakes-Dobson is a drama teacher and lecturer with an Honour's in Drama from the University of Cape Town. She has taught, directed and produced theatrical productions across all spectrums and ages.

Candice is married with a daughter, Annabel, whose real-life miniature horse is the hero of the *Pancakes* books. This is the third in the series, following *A Little Horse Called Pancakes* and *A Little Horse Called Pancakes And The Big Mountain Fire*. Sales of the books raise valuable funds for SARDA, a cause that is particularly close to Candice's heart.

Wendy Paterson is a mother, teacher and illustrator who lives near the foot of Table Mountain in Cape Town with her husband, two daughters, cat, guinea pig and rabbits. She is inspired by the endless patterns and colours in nature, and the funny things that children and animals say and do.

Published by Two Pups, an imprint of Burnet Media

First published 2017
1 3 5 7 9 8 6 4 2

ISBN 9781928230526

Text © 2017 Candice Noakes-Dobson
Illustrations © 2017 Wendy Paterson

Burnet Media | TWO PUPS

A special thank you to:

My Loving Parents – Tim & Marilyn Noakes
Editor Extraordinaire – Catriona Ross
Designer Magician – Maryse Collins
Publishing Guide – Tim Richman

The real Anna B and Pancakes.

Find them on Facebook:
@pancakesbookcollection